Herbster Readers

A FORT TO SHARE

Written by Joanne Meier and Cecilia Minden • Illustrated by Bob Ostrom
Created by Herbie J. Thorpe

ABOUT THE AUTHORS

Joanne Meier, PhD, has worked as an elementary school teacher, university professor, and researcher. She earned her BA in early childhood education from the University of South Carolina, and her MEd and PhD in education from the University of Virginia. She currently works as a literacy consultant for schools and private organizations. Joanne lives in Virginia with her husband Eric, daughters Kella and Erin, two cats, and a gerbil.

Cecilia Minden, PhD, is the former director of the Language and Literacy Program at the Harvard Graduate School of Education. She is now a reading consultant for school and library publications. She earned her PhD in reading education from the University of Virginia. Cecilia and her husband, Dave Cupp, live outside Chapel Hill, North Carolina. They enjoy sharing their love of reading with their grandchildren, Chelsea and Qadir.

ABOUT THE ILLUSTRATOR

Bob Ostrom has been illustrating children's books for nearly twenty years. A graduate of the New England School of Art & Design at Suffolk University, Bob has worked for such companies as Disney, Nickelodeon, and Cartoon Network. He lives in North Carolina with his wife Melissa and three children, Will, Charlie, and Mae.

ABOUT THE SERIES CREATOR

Herbie J. Thorpe had long envisioned a beginning-readers' series about a fun, energetic bear with a big imagination. Herbie is a book lover and an avid supporter of libraries and the role they play in fostering the love of reading. He consults with librarians and matches them with the perfect books for their students and patrons. He lives in Louisiana with his wife Misty and their daughter Carson.

The Child's World

Published in the United States of America by The Child's World®
1980 Lookout Drive • Mankato, MN 56003-1705
800-599-READ • www.childsworld.com

Acknowledgments
The Child's World®: Mary Berendes, Publishing Director
The Design Lab: Kathleen Petelinsek, Design;
Gregory Lindholm, Page Production
Colorist: Richard Carbajal

Library of Congress Cataloging-in-Publication Data
Meier, Joanne D.
 A fort to share / Joanne Meier and Cecilia Minden ; illustrated by Bob Ostrom.
   p. cm. — (Herbster readers)
 Summary: "In this simple story belonging to the second level of Herbster Readers, young Herbie and his friends build a fort and must learn to cooperate to get the job done."—Provided by publisher.
 ISBN 978-1-60253-012-6 (library bound : alk. paper)
 [1. Cooperativeness—Fiction. 2. Bears—Fiction.] I. Minden, Cecilia. II. Ostrom, Bob, ill. III. Title.
 PZ7.M5148For 2008
 [E]—dc22   2008002595

Herbie Bear wanted to build a fort.

Wildcats

Knock, knock!

It was Hank, Michael, and Hannah.

"Hi, guys! Want to build a fort?"

"Sure!" they said.

Everyone went to gather supplies.

Michael had boxes.

Hannah had a blanket.

Hank had a chair.

Everyone wanted to make their own fort.

"This isn't working!" said Herbie.

"Let's share! Then we can make one big fort."

Michael shared his boxes.

They made a great base.

Hannah shared her blanket.

It was a perfect roof.

Hank shared his chair.

It was a good door.

They all looked around.

"Where's Herbie?"

Herbie carried a plate of peanut-butter cookies.

"Let's share these, too!" said Herbie.
And they did.